Alice Schertle

Gus Wanders Off

Illustrated by Cheryl Harness

Lothrop, Lee & Shepard Books · New York

E
Sch

First Edition 1 2 3 4 5 6 7 8 9 10

Library or Congress Cataloging in Publication Data

Schertle, Alice. Gus wanders off.
Summary: Forgetting his mother's instructions, Gus leaves his yard to follow
his teacher's dog on an eventful walk through town, only to forget his way
home. [1. Lost children—Fiction. 2. Dogs—Fiction]
I. Harness, Cheryl ill.   II. Title.   PZ7.S3442Gu   [E]   86-21311
ISBN 0-688-04984-2   ISBN 0-688-04985-0 (lib. bdg.)

For Viv and Milt

A.S.

For Pam

C.H.

G us was playing in the front yard while Mama raked leaves. When the phone rang, Mama said, "Stay right here, Gus. Don't wander off."

Gus certainly didn't mean to wander off. But along came a curly burly dog that Gus had seen before. It belonged to Mrs. Bundy, his teacher. Sometimes she brought her curly burly dog to school.

"Hi, Hannibal," said Gus, and before he knew it he was following the dog's wag-a-lag tail down the street.

They passed Mrs. Biggs's house.
They passed Mr. Palmer's house.
Mr. and Mrs. Dinwiddie were sitting on their front
porch, soaking up the sun.

Gus and Mrs. Bundy's dog walked around the corner and into the park. They sat down together on the warm grass.

Gus couldn't quite tell if Hannibal was smiling, but Hannibal's long red tongue hung out in a very friendly way. Gus smiled and hung his tongue out, too.

Pretty soon Gus's tongue felt dry, and he went to get a drink from the water fountain. He put his finger on the spout and gave a drink to the curly burly dog.

Then Hannibal was on his way again, and Gus was following after that wag-a-lag tail.

Two big boys were playing basketball in the school yard. The ball came rolling across the yard, so Gus picked it up. He meant to throw it back to the boys, but it slipped out of his hands and dropped at his feet. That made the big boys laugh.

Gus and the curly burly dog walked on.

FISH SEAFOOD

FRESH CATFISH TODAY!

COME IN and TRY OUR GUMBO made fresh daily

OYSTERS and SALMON

OPEN

Down the street and around the corner they came
to a fish market with a row of trash cans in front.
Hannibal sniffed and snuffed around the cans until he
knocked one over.

A lot of paper and some fish heads fell out. Gus didn't
think the fish heads smelled very good, but the curly burly
dog must have thought they did, because he ate one.

Then off he trotted, and Gus followed right behind. They passed a barber shop, a bookstore, a bakery, and a music store.

"Hannibal!" cried a voice. "Where have you been? And Gus! Where did you come from?" Gus's teacher hurried across the street.

The curly burly dog put his big paws on Mrs. Bundy's shoulders and licked her with his long red tongue.

"Ugh!" said Mrs. Bundy. "You smell awful, Hannibal. What have you been into?"

"He ate a fish's head," Gus explained. "Even the eyeballs."

Mrs. Bundy shook her finger at the curly burly dog. "I told you never, never, never to wander off!"

Suddenly Gus got an uncomfortable feeling that he had forgotten something important. What was it Mama had said to him? *Stay right here, Gus. Don't wander off.*

"I have to go home," said Gus.

"Where do you live, Gus?" asked Mrs. Bundy.

Gus thought for a minute. "Forty-two eleven," he said.

"Forty-two eleven what?" asked Mrs. Bundy.

"I forget," said Gus.

"Well, you show me the way," said Mrs. Bundy. "Hannibal and I will walk with you."

So Gus and his teacher and her curly burly dog walked down a street or two and around a corner or two. But they must have been the wrong streets, or the wrong corners, because none of the houses looked like Gus's house. Gus began to feel worried.

"Can you think of something you saw as you walked along?" suggested Mrs. Bundy.

Gus did some hard thinking. "I remember the fish store. Hannibal knocked over the garbage can."

"That's where we'll go," said Mrs. Bundy. "You'll
remember the way from there."

But at the fish market Gus looked up the street and
down the street, and he couldn't exactly remember
which was the way home.

Gus thought some more. "I saw two big guys playing basketball," he said. "That ball was too heavy."

"Let's try the school yard," said Mrs. Bundy. "You'll remember the way from there."

At the school Gus looked up the street and down the street. How he hoped to see his own front yard! But none of the yards looked like Gus's yard.

"I remember the park," he said. "I gave Hannibal a drink."

"Good boy," said Mrs. Bundy, and off they went.

When they got to the park, Gus looked up the street and down the street, and there on the corner was a house he knew.

"There's the Dinwiddies' house!" he shouted.
"Do you live on Tuckernuck?" asked Mrs. Bundy.
"*Tuckernuck!*" cried Gus. "Forty-two eleven
Tuckernuck Avenue!"

Gus and Hannibal and Mrs. Bundy hurried past the Dinwiddies' house. Gus could see Mr. Palmer's house and Mrs. Biggs's house.

When Gus saw his own house, he began to run. And there was Mama, running up Tuckernuck Avenue to meet him.

Mama scooped Gus up in her arms and squeezed him tight. She thanked Mrs. Bundy for helping Gus find his way home.

"I was so worried," said Mama. "Promise me, Gus, that you'll never, never wander off again."

"I promise," said Gus.

Hannibal's wag-a-lag tail bounced back and forth, back and forth, as if to say, "Me too!"